Helen Hurts

Denise Fuchko and Keri Fuchko

Denise Fuchko   *Keri Fuchko*

FriesenPress

One Printers Way
Altona, MB R0G 0B0
Canada

www.friesenpress.com

ISBN
978-1-03-911743-3 (Hardcover)
978-1-03-911742-6 (Paperback)
978-1-03-911744-0 (eBook)

Juvenile Fiction, Health & Daily Living, Diseases, Illnesses & Injuries

Distributed to the trade by The Ingram Book Company

Dedicated to Finley

Helen hurts!

She wants the pain to magically **disappear.**

Helen was sick and needed an operation. The doctors and nurses in the hospital gave her medicine to help with the pain.
Mommy and Daddy gave her hugs and kisses.
Her friends sent cards and balloons, but Helen

still hurts.

On Monday, Mommy brought Helen a sparkly magic wand with a purple ribbon on it. Together they waved the wand and the room started to glow.

They chanted,

"Abracadabra, abracadabra, pain be gone,"

but that didn't work.

There was no magic solution for her pain.

On Tuesday morning, Helen woke up with a headache.

The doctor said, "Sometimes when we have

big feelings

it can cause a headache. Are you afraid?"
She nodded yes and the doctor wiped Helen's tears.

The doctor said, **"It's okay to feel scared.**

Sometimes feeling the emotions of fear and sadness
can cause the body to hurt. Pain can be very tricky.

Let's try singing."

Together they sang "Baby Shark."

After breakfast on Wednesday, Helen
yawned and stretched and that hurt.

The nurse said,

"Not all pain is bad.
Healing pain is there to remind you to be careful."

He told Helen some jokes and that made her laugh.

A physical therapist came to visit Helen in the afternoon. Helen had never met a physical therapist before and was unsure how she could help. The physical therapist said it was her job to help people move better so they can get back to doing the things they love.

She taught Helen to notice where she tightens her body when she feels pain. The physical therapist showed her ways to lessen the tension in her body by tightening and relaxing the muscles of one body part at a time. Helen started to feel better as they went from the top of her head to the tips of her toes.

Why did the cookie go to the doctor?
It felt CRUMMY!
What can you CATCH but never THROW?
A COLD!

On Thursday, Helen went home. It was raining. Daddy said, "Let's pretend we are camping. I can hear the rain on our tent.

Pitter-patter, pitter-patter, pitter-patter

Can you hear it?"

Helen nodded yes.

"Imagine we are cosy in our comfortable sleeping bags. Remember when it was so cold we could see our breath? Let's see if we can see our breath as we breathe deeply. Let's count to three.

Breathe in . . . 1, 2, 3, and breathe out . . . 1, 2, 3. In . . . 1, 2, 3, and out . . . 1, 2, 3."

Helen cuddled close to Daddy; she relaxed and fell asleep.

On Friday afternoon, Helen's pain came back,

but it wasn't as bad.

Grandma came for a visit. Together they snuggled under a soft striped blanket on the big blue couch. They read her favourite books. Helen told Grandma when she forgot a word.

She imagined herself in the story,
floating on the cotton candy clouds.

On Saturday, her pain returned. Grandpa came for a visit.

"Let's go outside to the garden for some fresh air," suggested Grandpa.

Helen thought it was a good idea. They
blew bubbles. Grandpa said,

"When the bubbles pop, imagine popping your pain."

Helen thought Grandpa was silly and giggled.

ABCDEFG...HIJK...LMNOP...QRS...TUV...W...X...Y and Z...Now I know my ABC's...Next time won't yoyu sing with me....ABCDEFG..HIJKLMNOP...QRSTUV...WXY... and Z...Now I know my ABC's...Next time won't yoyu sing with me!

Sunday night, Helen was lying in her bed. She had a little pain. Softly, she sang her ABCs. Helen hugged her favourite teddy and stroked his furry face.

She whispered, "I am safe and loved."

Helen pretended she was on her floaty at the lake.
She could almost hear the blue jay calls from the tall fir trees.

She relaxed her face, arms, stomach, and legs. She imagined it
was hot and sunny. Helen began to feel **calm and peaceful.**

**She started breathing slowly:
in and out, in and out.**

Her pain gradually disappeared.
Helen sighed and smiled.

She felt powerful!

Note to Parents and Caregivers

Pain is our body's warning system and its job is to protect us. It is important children know their pain is believed, especially if there is no clear cause for it. If we can learn ways to calm the body, we can help decrease the pain experienced.

Introducing children to a variety of pain management strategies is important. Depending on how they are feeling, they may prefer different strategies. The more children practice these techniques when they are well, the easier it will be for them to implement when they are feeling unwell.

Please refer to the resources provided for more information, or talk to a health care professional if you have specific questions about your child's pain.

Here is a brief summary of the various evidence-informed strategies introduced in *Helen Hurts*:

Strategy	Example(s) in Book	Potential Benefits
Breathwork	Counting and breathing Blowing bubbles Slow breaths	↓ **Pain** ↓ **Stress** ↑ **Relaxation**
Distraction	Reading, cuddling Blowing bubbles	↓ **Anxiety** ↑ **Coping skills**
Humor	Telling jokes	↓ **Tension** ↓ **Emotional distress** ↑ **Coping**
Guided imagery	Pretending to camp Popping bubbles of pain	↓ **Anxiety** ↓ **Pain**
Mind–Body techniques	Mindfulness (noticing sounds, sensations, and feelings) Positive affirmations Progressive Muscle Relaxation	↓ **Pain** ↓ **Muscle tension** ↓ **Anxiety** ↑ **Coping** ↑ **Relaxation**
Music	Singing "Baby Shark"	↓ **Anxiety** ↓ **Pain**
Pain Education	"Healing pain is there to remind you to be careful" and "Sometimes feeling the emotions of fear sadness can cause the body to hurt."	↓ **Unhelpful beliefs** ↓ **Pain** ↓ **Fear associated with pain**

Online resources to learn more about managing children's pain:

1. **Meg Foundation** – A foundation harnessing the power of technology to empower kids and families to prevent and relieve pain.
https://www.megfoundationforpain.org/
Instagram: @megfoundationforpain

2. **The Comfort Ability** – A program to help kids, teens, and caregivers learn how to better manage chronic pain.
https://www.thecomfortability.com/
Instagram: @thecomfability

3. **SKIP** – A collaborative network of scientists, health care workers, and parents working to improve children's pain management.
https://kidsinpain.ca/
Instagram: @kidsinpain

4. **AboutKidHealth** – An educational website with general information about pain for children, youth, and their caregivers.
https://www.aboutkidshealth.ca/pain

5. **Easing the Ouch** – Accessible information backed by science to empower children and adults to manage their pain.
Instagram: @easingtheouch

CPSIA information can be obtained
at www.ICGtesting.com
Printed in the USA
BVHW060602051221
622833BV00002B/8

9 781039 117426